ANTHOLOGY
OF HUMOROUS
SANSKRIT
VERSES

ANTHOLOGY OF HUMOROUS SANSKRIT VERSES

A.N.D. HAKSAR

PENGUIN BOOKS

An imprint of Penguin Random House

PENGUIN BOOKS

USA | Canada | UK | Ireland | Australia
New Zealand | India | South Africa | China

Penguin Books is part of the Penguin Random House group of companies
whose addresses can be found at global.penguinrandomhouse.com

Published by Penguin Random House India Pvt. Ltd
4th Floor, Capital Tower 1, MG Road,
Gurugram 122 002, Haryana, India

First published in Penguin Books by Penguin Random House India 2022

English translation and Introduction copyright © A.N.D. Haksar 2022

All rights reserved

10 9 8 7 6 5 4 3 2 1

ISBN 9780670095827

Typeset in Adobe Garamond Pro by Manipal Technologies Limited, Manipal
Printed at Replika Press Pvt. Ltd, India

www.penguin.co.in

P.M.S

For my dear daughter
Sharada
with all my love

Contents

Introduction

This collection is intended to provide the interested reader with some glimpses of the humorous sentiment or *hasya rasa* in ancient Sanskrit literature, an aspect not too well known in present times.

For many centuries, this great literature has come to be associated mainly with religion and philosophy, rituals of worship, and the retelling of myths and legends. Some didactic material from it on public and private life and some from literary classics is also known and studied. However, several other dimensions of this wide-ranging literature are now little known.

An over 2000-year-old treatise on the subject, the *Natya Shastra* of Bharata categorized eight *rasas* or sentiments evoked in Sanskrit drama and poetry. One of them was humorous (*hasya*). The others were erotic (*shringara*), heroic (*vira*), furious (*raudra*), fearful (*bhayanaka*), compassionate (*karuna*), marvellous (*adbhuta*) and horrific (*bibhatsa*). Calmness and peace (*shanta*) were later added to this list. Several scholars provided quotations from the classics to illustrate all nine sentiments, although those on *hasya* were usually fewer.

Still-studied ancient experts such as Anandavardhana, the ninth century author of *Dhvanyaloka*, and Mammata, the eleventh century writer of *Kavyaprakasa*, exemplified all *rasas* with quotations from the *Vedas* and other scriptures as well as some *mahakavyas* or great poetic works. However, since such texts were not easily available for general readers, later experts began the practice of compiling verse anthologies of such poetry for a larger public readership. Several of these appeared over the last millennium and are still available today.

The collection presented here is largely of direct translations of selected verses from some of these still-respected medieval anthologies of Sanskrit verses. These are the thirteenth-century *Sukti Muktavali* (Pearl String of Verses) from the Deccan, the fourteenth-century *Sarngadhara Paddhati* (Guide of Sarngadhara) from Rajasthan, and the sixteenth-century *Subhashitavali* (Garland of Well-Said Verses) from Kashmir. A fourth, *Subhashita Ratna Bhandagara* (Treasury of Verse Gems) is the largest and dates a little later from present-day Maharashtra. The fifth is *Chittavinodini* (Mental Recreation), a recent compilation from Lucknow from about a hundred years ago. Some samples have also been taken from a recent work named *Hasyarnava* (Sea of Humour) and from a later book entitled *Humour in Sanskrit Literature*. Details of all these are given in the notes below. Other old anthologies were also consulted, although they did not have the requisite material.

The verses presented here reflect ancient humour that deserves more exposure to readers today. Some verses make fun even of gods and religion. Some are quotations from the Gita and other parts of the Mahabharata. Many display wit and sarcasm, earthy humour and cynical satire, though mostly in a mild and gentle manner. All are epigrammatic, expressing sentiment in a single stanza, and are easy to hear, remember or read. Such simple poetry in various *rasas* attracted a wider audience, thereby leading to the compilation of anthologies. For ease of reading, this one has been presented in a number of short cantos of self-explanatory and independent verses, with some of their sources marked at the end of each and a few further details presented in the bibliography.

The selection and translation of this collection have brought me much peace and joy, especially during the pandemic. My thanks are due to Penguin and to their Classics Editor Ananya Bhatia for accepting the proposal for this book, to her successor Rea Mukherjee for its editing and publication and also to Aparna Abhijit, its copy editor.

Note to the Introduction

1. Jalhana, *Sukti Muktavali* (Devagiri, c. 1257)
2. *Sarngadhara Paddhati* (Jaipur, c. 1363)
3. Vallabhdeva, *Subhashitavali* (Kashmir, c. 16th century)
4. *Subhashita Ratna Bhandagara* (Bombay: Nirnaya Sagar Press, 1891)
5. *Chittavinodini*, ed. R.N. Ghosh (Lucknow, 1938)
6. Jagadiswara Bhattachaarya, *Hasyarnava Prahasana*, ed. I.P. Chaturvedi (Varanasi: Chaukhamba Vidyabhavan, 1969)
7. C. Shivaraju, *Humour in Sanskrit Literature* (Mumbai: Himalaya Publishing House, Mumbai, 2003)

Canto 1

Subhashitavali (Su.) and others

Oh, the goddess Lakshmi sees
Krishna playing with the cows,
and being to her spouse devoted,
she does always take the side
of people who have bovine minds.   1   *Su. v. 2291*

When his garb is simple space,
why does he need garments?
If he is covered in ashes,
what for any woman?
And if he does have a woman,
why hate Kama, God of Love?
Seeing all these contradictions
in the ways of his master Shiva,
the body of his servant Bhringi
is just a skeletal bag of bones.   2   *Su. v. 2399*

Fearing that the colour she has used
may then get washed off her lips,
that wanton woman, near a well,
though she is extremely thirsty,
will not drink the water there.   3   *Su. v. 2336*

He cannot read what others write,
his own script no one can read:
the curious thing about him is
that he himself cannot decipher
that of which he is the writer.   4   *Su. v. 2334*

Most holy is this sacred cord,
and holding it in my priestly hand,
I do swear this oath—
there is nothing so charming as
those women with beauteous bottoms,
or a greater source of pain.   5   *Su. v. 2389*

Today, to folk who sing their praise,
kings are like wish-fulfilling trees
that always bear them fruit;
but good people only get,
at the time of evening prayers,
some things small, like bits of camphor,
offered to the lamp at worship.   6   *Su. v. 2395*

First a housemaid, then a call-girl,
she later became a procuress;
but now, devoid of all these means,
an ascetic has that old whore turned.   7   *SP v. 4052*

These six live on the following six,
no seventh one is there;
thieves subsist on careless people,
doctors on those who are ill,
women on libidinous men,
priests on folk who come for prayers,
and on litigants do the rulers live,
as learned *pandits* do on fools.   8   *Mahabharata 5.33*

That monk eats meat with greatest pleasure,
but what is it without some wine?
And what indeed is wine without
the company of courtesans?
But prostitutes do relish money,
and where is wealth without recourse
to some trick or thievery?   9   *Dasarupaka*

In that darkness dense, one cannot
have delight that is the sight
of the arching of her eyebrows;
nor can there be any talk
with some sweet exchange of words;
and, for fear of being seen,
the heart too isn't fully satisfied.
Even so, how strange it is,
that one can have tremendous pleasure
in making love, like a thief, in secret.   10   *Su. v. 2380*

In the course of sex, there may be pain,
for the lips and hair, for the breasts and thighs,
but for the zone betwixt their legs,
there is pleasure for the lovers,
as there is for orators
taking part in a great debate.   11   *Su. v. 2347*

That clerk is like a serpent
in the puddle which is the court;
he kills folk with his fangs, the pen
dipped in the poison of his ink.   12   *Narma Mala*

He is indeed a lord supreme,
that illustrious bureaucrat
who can delude the world entire
with illusions of his will
and, without suffering defeat,
is always victorious.   13   *Narma Mala*

He tricks even the God of Death,
with his notes that are so negative,
and his weapon is a pen
that even celestials suspect.   14   *Su. v. 2325*

Kayastha means 'government official'—
who could have this word invented
with first syllables of three others:
kaka or a greedy crow,
yama or the pitiless God of Death,
and *sthapaka* or maker of things?   15   *Su. v. 2324*

Canto 2

Sarngadhara Paddhati (SP) and others

This is as clear as clear can be:
her name means the mountain's daughter,
his the trunk of a leafless tree;
they are both always joined together,
but are without any desire
for making love and its felicity.   1   *Su. v. 2314*

One who looks for some atonement
for being by his darling kicked,
his head then deserves a wash
with a mouthful of some wine
from that girl, for purification.   2   *Su. v. 2392*

My night was like a terrible death
in pretending to make love
with a young and artless *brahman*,
his body rough with constant labour,
and for whom a girl is hard to get.   3   *Su. v. 2339*

It's a common saying, but quite untrue,
that cracks or holes cause many problems:
for sensual women they do not,
but can bring rewards of pleasure.   4   *Su. v. 2351*

For some it seems to crack the teeth,
stifle taste and split the palate,
and make the throat contract:
such is the pure and lovely water
poured from jars, now cold become
with the winter wind, unbearable,
that these unfortunate people
simply have to drink each day.   5   *Su. v. 2372*

Our Creator has designed
a thing which is so useful
for concealing ignorance
and in one's own hands,
especially in the company
of those who know everything:
for people who are ignorant,
silence is the best adornment.   6   *Su. v. 2382*

'Having come to Dwaraka,
we spend the day in worshipping Hari
and, viewing life as a holy fast,
release ourselves in the holy river.'
'Now, spending every morning in
such a tale of indifference,
O harlots, may you have the pleasure
of endless love-making at night!'   7   *SP v. 4054*

My lips have been purified
by singing a *Vedic* hymn;
do not, dear girl, dirty them,
but if eager for some enjoyment,
then do nibble my left ear!   8   *SP v. 4062*

With a start of unclear murmurings,
then words of praise for the invitation
and pleasing ones about himself:
thus does that singer sing his song.   9   *SP v. 4048*

The poor thief does get frightened by
shouts coming from the dark,
but that singer, crook and fraud,
is by shouts never embarrassed.   10   *SP v. 4047*

Far away is the mountain Meru:
it has abandoned human lands
as it is afraid of robbery
by those thieves, the goldsmiths.   11   *SP v. 4049*

There need not ever be a king
for robbers and bandits,
as the goldsmith singly
does always punish them all.   12   *SP v. 4050*

Gesturing with his fingers,
his lips muttering prayers,
his scholarship involved in
many kinds of arguments,
that city leader is absorbed
in being with the people.   13   *SP v. 4029*

Cleverness in weighing goods
in purchase or sale
and tricks for confiscating deposits:
thus do they, these day-time robbers,
the traders steal from people.   14   *SP v. 4035*

Get some food, O foolish mind,
be merciful to life:
it is there from birth to birth,
but another's food is hard to get.   15   *SP v. 4034*

Canto 3

Su. and SP, as in Canto 1 and Humour in Sanskrit Literature (HSL)

Your body's lustre, age still young,
unfettered worldly sovereignty:
all this, O king, you want to give up
for a cause that thoughtless seems to be,
and trifling too appears to me.   1   *HSL p. 15*

'The sandal powder on my body
is made of ashes from a fire,
my garland is the sacred thread,
a string of beads, my jewelled bracelet,
and my silken garments are
just barks taken off a tree':
thus did Ravana imagine
he would attract the eyes of Sita.   2   *HSL p. 20*

You speak words of wisdom, but
grieve for those who need no grief:
as wise people do not mourn,
either for those already gone
or others who yet have not.   3   *Gita 2.11*

He spends half the morning
washing his stool, while discussing
with gentle folk some royal rumours;
his hands are then busy collecting
some sacred grass and flowers;
thereafter that holy ascetic,
on the pretext of doing yoga,
takes off all his garments
while his vision is immersed
in gazing at young women's breasts.   4   *SP v. 4028*

Like the moon he is in looks,
as a cuckoo in his voice,
like a pigeon he kisses, like a swan he moves,
and crushes a girl in his embrace,
as could do an elephant:
such is my husband, with all merits
that young women admire.
There is no defect, but if there are
difficulties, then they must be
that he is married to me.   5   *Su. v. 2386*

When the dental consonants
cannot be properly pronounced,
always, when that person speaks,
the only difference that there is
between his mouth and the nether hole
is that the second has no teeth.   6   *Su. v. 2397*

The aged and those full of youth,
the low-born and patrician folk,
the weak and sick, and those strong-bodied:
in all these are the spirits same,
in yogis and in harlots too.   7   *HSL p. 12,*

Love on lips, but not in the heart,
arms upright, but not the nature,
breasts well set, but not behaviour:
the latter good folk never applaud.   8   *HSL p. 12*

In the hands, a copper cup,
and on the palms, some sacred grass,
clad in robes well washed and white,
with a clay *tilak* on the forehead,
and on it a flower blossom
that is dipped in sandal juice,
then with long strides and a firm gait,
and a voice clipped within his teeth:
in such ways that holy trickster
does deceive the world.   9   *SP v. 4021*

Hairy body, piercing eyes,
crooked eyebrows on the forehead,
in huge gulps that hungry *brahman*,
swallows large mouthfuls of rice.   10   *SP v. 4032*

What crimes have your hair committed?
Shave off anger from your head.
What need is there of monkish colours
when the mind itself is saffron-tinted?   11   *Su. v. 2294*

As workers have to tolerate
of long distances the fatigue,
the people who get sold as slaves
the weights they have to carry,
and folk suffering from ailments
the misery of bitter medicines:
so do women put up with
living in their in-laws' houses.   12   *Su. v. 2394*

I'm pushed around by my mother-in-law,
so too by her daughter,
also by the young brother-in-law;
even so, dear friend, I stay
in that house to have the pleasure
of being near my husband.   13   *Su. v. 2396*

Friend, listen to this curious deed
done on me by a rustic client:
my eyes were shut in feeling pleasure,
he was afraid that I was dead
and released me straightaway.   14   *SP v. 4058*

Whores love a client praising them,
or one for his cash and treasure,
another for service or protection,
and yet another just for pleasure.   15   *SP v. 4053*

Canto 4

also from Subhashita Ratna Bhandagara (SRB)

Lakshmi sleeps on a lotus blossom,
Shiva on a hill of snow,
and Vishnu sleeps on a sea of milk.
I think this is because they are all worried
about the bed bugs where they lie.   1   *SRB Hasya*

In a world that is so worthless,
the father-in-law's abode alone
is a worthy place:
so Hara rests in the Himalayas,
and Hari in the ocean.   2   *SRB Hasya*

Lying in her husband's arms,
the sweet words that she spoke at night,
their mynah bird her voice imitating,
next morning said before the parents,
and embarrassed the bride.   3   *Su. v. 2162*

Her breasts stand out,
the middle is sunken,
the hips are very prominent:
who indeed on such a body
of that girl with fawn-like eyes,
will not trip and slip?   4   *Su. v. 1268*

It is not fit to carry weight
or in the field to pull a plough,
but this bull in the temple courtyard
can still eat very well.   5   *Su. v. 953*

She hindered their intercourse,
made joyless their talk together,
so that her lover, full of passion,
suddenly then did fall asleep.   6   *Su. v. 2050*

You are soft, but they are hard,
big and round, while you are slim;
you are shy, but they look bold:
such are the breasts outside your heart.   7   *SP v. 334*

Make love, lover, while you may,
for your youth is passing away.
When you are dead, who will give you,
with the funeral, a sweet cunt too?   8   *Su. v. 2366*

There is no fear of the palate cracking,
or splitting of the tongue;
therefore, in indiscriminate chatter,
which shameless person is not skilled?   9   *SRB Hasya*

With no meat or liquor,
nor robbery from others,
or causing them injury,
that official weeps all day.   10   *SRB Hasya*

Though shaving hair is just the same,
see—here is a difference:
insects eat those of the pelvis,
and heads shaved, ascetics enjoy *ghee*.   11   *SRB Hasya*

He loves stories, always goes
to hear the holy books recited,
but runs away from doing works
as if bitten by a black serpent.   12   *SRB Hasya*

Covering himself as do timid petitioners,
and looking out in all directions
like a thief, that wicked fellow
by a crooked road does run away.   13   *SRB Hasya*

The goddess of the state's prosperity
sadly weeps, tears darkened by
ink drops trickling from the pen
of that clerk who plundered her.   14   *SRB Hasya*

All the work that people do
is indeed to make a living,
but it is destroyed by goat-like voices
of the rogues who are the singers.   15   *SRB Hasya*

Canto 5

from Sukti Muktavali (SM) (HP) of Jalhana

Those widows with large and lovely breasts—
in cheating them with words intended
their discontent to pacify
and showering them with holy advice,
some rogues always take the pleasure
of kissing them long and fearlessly.   1   *SM* (*HP v. 9*)

As just a girl, sometimes as a servant,
as a hired woman or a whore—
O friend, she is thus long regarded,
even though another's wife:
the wishes in one's inner mind
are never satisfied.   2   *SM* (*HP v. 12*)

No learning or eloquence,
not even any craftiness;
how can you then have, minister
the feeling of not being rewarded?   3   *SM* (*HP v. 13*)

You wear a sage's robe, O fool,
hard even for an ass to carry.
What of the weight you have to bear
of long hair and the sacred cords?   4   *SM* (*HP v. 15*)

In her way of showing love,
his follower, an aged woman,
did offer her lips to him.
But that Buddhist monk declined,
saying, 'This is like eating meat, O beauty—
not permissible at this time.'   5   *SM (HP v. 17)*

Dislike of the loyal, for the stupid, love,
a nature to disregard the good,
and always saying bitter words—
such are the rich and those who are sick.   6   *SM (HP v. 27)*

Having bathed in the sea,
he sits on the shore before the people—
that ascetic, his body draped
in a saffron-coloured robe,
thinking where to get as alms
some broth mixed with honey and butter,
in the houses of young women
whose husbands have gone away.   7   *SM (HP v. 14)*

Face like a monkey, arms like vines,
the belly like a drum,
the waist no more than a fistful—
thus, O beauty, is your body.   8   *SM (HP v. 25)*

As it proclaims authority,
hear the words of the drum:
'Bound and empty, with sticks beaten,
like me you will become.'   9   *SM* (*HP v. 30*)

No caresses of her hair,
no joyful embrace of the breasts,
no method for kissing each limb,
or apt words for a game of sex—
that man, it's clear, is a labourer
in making love to a housewife.   10   *SM* (*HP v. 33*)

'I do not thirst for heaven's delights,
nor ever pray or beg for things,
for I am always satisfied
with just living on twigs.'
'But sir, this is not fit for you.
If folk could go to heaven without
the prayers that are said for them,
why do friends and children then
do so for their mothers and fathers?'   11   *SM* (*HP v. 51*)

He looks at it with sympathy—
the face of a girl from a good family
who does sigh with trembling eyes.
He feels the plump and bristling limbs,
shyly exposed by a whore
and removes, with heated water,
a eunuch's wealth long gathered.
Such are a doctor's arts and learning
that are the store of all his pleasure,
and deserve to be saluted.   12   *SM* (*HP v. 31*)

They move about, embraced by others;
sometime stumble on the way,
and also speak unclearly—
like drunkards are those wealthy folk.   13   *SM* (*HP v. 29*)

That shameless and saucy man,
struck by a current of desire,
does cohabit with a young woman,
her hips disrobed upon the bed,
and the job of Kama done,
does leave that house immediately.   14   *SM* (*HP v. 42*)

The merchant gets up with a bow,
greets one and offers his seat,
and seeing a hand that may give enough,
starts a cordial conversation.   15 *SM* (*HP v. 40*)

Canto 6

from Jalhana SM, HP

'What is it, mother, on top of his head?'
'Son, it is the crescent moon.'
'And what is that upon his forehead?'
'That is his flaming eye.'
'What's in his throat?' 'It's a poison.'
'And that thing below his navel?'
Hearing from her son this last,
Parvati covers his eyes
and puts her hand upon his mouth.
May she protect us always.   1   *SM HP v. 1*

That courtesan is a wealthy woman—
she makes arrangements with great merit,
and gets of areca nuts a horde
to use as a paste for body massage,
what to say of grating other nuts
for lubricants in making love,
while soft coverings of China silk
also in that process gleam.   2   *SM HP v. 4*

That guru had practiced breath control,
also on scriptures commented,
and at the time of his demise,
his blessings did come out like a fart.   3   *SM HP v. 20*

'One who digs a hundred holes
is, in my view, fully accomplished,
but one who makes a thousand such
is just losing all his vigour'—
thus does speak that man, a miner,
naked, filthy, rough and thin.   4   *SM HP v. 38*

One who makes things out of gold
himself treats his wealth as ash,
but all of it does get destroyed
by one who is an expert in cheating.   5   *SM HP v. 39*

Hard and sharp, like the edge of an axe
that cuts down the trees of love—
she has a mind given to blaming others,
looking at them with unkind eyes,
and does nothing the ground to moisten,
only hurling thunderbolts—
such is that procuress, a go-between.   6   *SM HP v. 48*

If by force he takes a girl,
poor, in bad times and on sale—
alas that young and penniless man
does it as an image of Kama;
for her door then is with iron bolted,
and that luckless maid stays awake for long. 7   *SM HP v. 45*

They see the sun in a lotus blossom,
in a blooming lily, the golden moon,
and the peacock in a clouded sky;
but rich doctors, like the hunters,
mostly have no joy within.   8   *SM HP v. 22*

Her hair is white, like a horde of cotton,
the breasts droop, touching Kama's abode,
and cheeks are marked with age-old wrinkles;
but even then, the courtesan
does not give up sex.   9   *SM HP v. 24*

O messenger girl, your mind
is as colourless as your lips—
both do show without pretence
the emptiness of all you say.   10   *SM 48.1*

Forgetting what I need, what more
can I tell you, messenger girl?
Have already given even my body—
what to say of other things?   11   *SM HP 48 v. 4*

O messenger girl, that man wants
just to get at my lips and me,
and with the slightness of his affection,
my mind has already become
placid, like water in a tank.   12   *SM HP 48*

You simple girl, my eyes have seen
on the buds, your lips, a blossoming smile—
there will be fruit, I do believe,
and now wish to tell you so.   13   *SM SP 3*

Seeing her power to revive
desire and also stem its waning,
the moon, home of ambrosia,
gleams on the pearl at her nose.   14   *SM SD 7*

O beauty, what is this archery
that you always display?
There is no bowstring, nor an arrow,
but hearts are pierced all the way!   15   *SM SP 18*

Canto 7

from SM HP and others

Both feet washed with his jug's water,
he puts on the ground with obscene grunts,
even as his fingers are all busy
in counting those unholy spells.   1   *SM HP v. 10*

Nights they pass in homes of whores,
sleepless, busy with feasts of love,
enjoying sips of those ladies' lips;
but in daytime, they are all-knowing,
ordained priests performing rites—
thus do those rogues deceive the world.   2   *SM HP v. 11*

They farm their land in timely rains,
but rain untimely pleases physicians—
the first increases crops of grain,
but the second spreads disease.   3   *SM HP v. 21*

Logic, brother, what's your meaning?
Analysis, friend, you can also cheat.
Vedas, dear, where are your blessings?
And in a bad way are you, O Poetry!
All of you are used by rogues
for spreading dominion of their rulers.   4   *SM HP v. 6*

In fear that it may fade away,
the colour that she has put on her lips,
that harlot weeps, 'O Father! Father!'
though her own is dead since long ago.   5   *SM HP v.41*

She looks at his eyes like flowers dear,
even though they are no more.
As with that old man, that aged woman
goes always to assuage his feelings.   6   *SM HP v. 32*

With fierce roars from warriors,
Like Karna, Shalya and Bhagadatta,
that army of the lord of Kurus
is like a merciless procuress.   7   *SM HP v. 47*

A plain woman who is not meticulous,
when moved may laugh softly;
she does not care for pilgrimage,
but makes attempts at fornication
with a wish to get some pleasure
for her body with big breasts,
a queen of hangers-on and servants—
may that whore bring luck for us.   8   *SM HP v. 3*

Her teeth twinkle like a row of jasmines,
her clothes are always washed and clean,
sweet of speech, she has nice lips
and a *tilaka* that does steal the heart,
and at night she is just like the moon—
but she speaks too much!   9   *SM HP v. 49*

'I bow to you, respected lady,
who has obtained the fruit of virtue
and a place in the *Jaina* heaven.
What else can I say, O learned one,
about my faith upon your mind?'
Hearing this, that nun smiled sweetly
as my gaze went down to her navel region. 10   *SM HP v. 19*

In time of rain, in fear of falling
and uneasy with this water,
can't one just in some place stand?
But friend, the roads are slippery too!   11   *SM Vakrokti*

That charming girl does not go home
but stays in someone else's house,
for someone told her that, this summer,
that traveller also will stay there.   12   *SM Vakrokti*

Her garland is an intestine,
some female palm, a blood red lotus,
that is suddenly worn as a chaplet,
and taking both, just given by her lover,
that demon girl then takes a drought
of grease, as wine from a skull, her cup. 13   *SM Bibhatsa 4*

They even stand in some hut's corner,
but never note the wealth of others;
for such, even this universe
can be put in a pail.   14   *SM Adbhuta 95*

May all poets quickly see
this wonder on a snowy hill crest
of that Lord of the Night—
with one hand he holds a silvery pot,
and with the other enacts a draught.   15 *SM Adbhuta 95*

Canto 8

from Subhashita Ratna Bhandagara (SRB)

Krishna his home remembers,
where he was so liberal-minded.
One spouse was of a singular nature,
the second was rather fickle,
his son, the God of Love, unstoppable,
could conquer all the world,
a snake-killing eagle was his mount,
and a serpent had become the bed
on which he slept in the ocean.   1   *SRB v. 47*

These six are the worst of men—
he who puts ashes on his fingers,
one tricky, like a flying crane,
he who claims to purify children,
one who just prays all the time,
he who lives by the edge of his sword,
and one who seeks to be a king.   2   *SRB v. 8*

One, who only orders others,
and he who just carries them out,
one faithless to his own profession,
and he who always leans on others,
one who says he is a yogi,
and one always sick, when ordered—
these six are the worst of servants.   3   *SRB v. 9*

The humble folk who go to awaken
one who sleeps like Kumbhakarna
may get blown off by the wind
discharged from his bottom.   4   *SRB v. 11*

Outside that burrow is the cat,
inside it is the serpent,
in between there glows a mouse,
like with two wives does a man.   5   *SRB v. 14*

He himself has faces five;
of his two sons, one is elephant-faced
and the other has visages six.
How would this naked one survive
without a giver of food at home
like the goddess Annapurna?   6   *SRB v. 16*

Now, afraid of filling two bellies,
half his body is that of the wife.
If the other part is not their son,
how is he still a celibate?   7   *SRB v. 17*

Moon-crested, mounted on a bull
and always with your spouse—
is this why you have, O Hara,
on your forehead another eye?   8   *SRB v. 36*

I wear this cloak just as a flower;
my father's limbs it had embellished,
was used by grandfather as a youth,
and will adorn my sons and grandsons.   9   *SRB v. 39*

Cheating them for long with words
that this won't affect their ascetic life,
but on the pretext of blessing them,
those rascals, with their juicy kisses,
dampen the cheeks and breasts of harlots.10   *SRB v. 40*

'Your hands, O whore, may be impure,
but my blessings will give them purity.
As such, now do massage my head.'
But on her tender strokes, that priest
Vishnu Sharma weeps and cries—
'Alas, alas, I have been hit!'   11   *SRB v. 43*

She is fair, fine eyes and nose,
a slim waist and a lovely skirt,
and limbs mostly smooth and hairless.
But as she asks about his pleasure,
her newly-wedded husband says,
'This is not all. Where is the rest?'   12   *SRB v. 44*

I am now old, the hair gone white,
my teeth have all decayed;
but this is not what makes me sad.
It is when young women, seeing me
then cry out, 'O Father! Father!'
That's like a strike by a thunderbolt.   13   *SRB v. 45*

O people, quickly close your ears
with your hands and be attentive,
as all the mountains on this earth
seem denser when Ravana
with a cloth does cover the nose
of this sleeping Kumbhakarna,
who then makes a terrible noise
by letting off a fearful fart.   14   *SRB v. 56*

It is not due to the father or mother
that Shambhu's son is called Gajanana;
it is like one who is declared a student
without any *Vedas* or other scriptures.   15   *SRB v. 37*

Canto 9

Sarngadhara Paddhati (SP)

Staring at some maiden's breasts,
that young man shakes his head
as if to extract his gaze
that is immersed between them.   1   *SP v. 3950*

Childhood spent getting educated,
youth in hunting, wealth amassing,
then the role of royal folk does turn
just to enjoy the bums of beauties.   2   *SP v. 3955*

Insects, ash or excrement,
and all kinds of anxiety—
these cause trouble to this body.
What's the way to be rid of them?   3   *SP v. 4141*

Her body is just flesh and blood—
to touch it may some pleasure give,
but really pretty it is not
for lions and others eat it too.   4   *SP v. 4142*

Seeing the whiteness of his hair
and other signs of that man's decline
that have left him just a bag of bones,
young women avoid him from afar,
like a well that is for outcasts meant.   5   *SP v. 4146*

The breasts are merely knots of flesh,
but are compared to golden bowls;
the mouth is just the abode of spit,
but like the moon is seen to be;
and thighs, made wet by urination,
are compared to elephants' trunks—
thus do clever poets make them special
things that are condemnable.   6   *SP v. 4147*

Though unripe, the fruit of mango
can be heated for a while
with jaggery and ginger paste
to make them quickly flow with juice.   7   *SP v. 3005*

'Beautiful, give up this pride.
Look, I am at your feet;
you have indeed never been
so angry as at this time!'
Her lover, having spoken thus,
she did then shed a few tears
from a corner of her half-shut eyes,
but said nothing at all.   8   *SP v. 3577*

At a drinking party, seeing
some wine in that woman's mouth,
Kama then came to give assistance
and seized her like Rahu does the moon.   9   *SP v. 3647*

The tinkle of her anklet bells
is silent; what is now heard
is that of the girdle on her hips
as her husband seeks some rest
and the girl now acts the man.   10   *SP v. 3696*

Her breasts do bounce,
the hair is undone,
sweat on the face and a soft smile—
it is for their special good deeds
that men may get a pretty girl
with qualities also masculine.   11   *SP v. 3698*

Soiled with sweat and excreta,
when urine flows out like some blood,
it is then from a terrible sore
that blinds all the world.   12   *SP v. 4079*

Can I bring ambrosia,
from the nether world?
Can I extract nectar from
a squeezing of the moon?
Can I avoid the heat produced
by drinking liquor strong?
Well, I can, if I now do quickly
plough this little bit of land.   13   *SP v. 4080*

For a moment, having been a child,
for another a pleasure-seeking youth,
for some time without any money,
at another with all of wealth—
now, with a body full of wrinkles
and all worn out by age,
man, like an actor, does retire
behind the curtains of this world.   14   *SP v. 4094*

Love is an oil that lubricates;
it also causes calamity.
This becomes quite obvious
from a lamp run out of oil.   15   *SP v. 4100*

Canto 10

Subhashitavali (Su.)

From your food, a drop of *ghee*
can even to a cat be given,
but a piece of chicken breast
for one's meal is hard to get.　　　　1　　*Su. v. 2312*

He may shout very loudly
and take deep breaths suddenly,
but if he speaks about hundreds of things,
at least listen to such a person.　　　2　　*Su. v. 2330*

Though his steps are soft, he's not a cat
or an ascetic, though he can hold his breath,
or a snake that always seeks some burrow,
nor god of death, holding a stick.   3   *Su. v. 2329*

They subsist on deaths and corpses,
some money-earning from last rites,
but when their intents are unfulfilled,
that is what upholds the world.   4   *Su. v. 2322*

He sings hymns that have no metre
and verses strung with vulgar words;
even so, he practices them—
such are the merits of that prince.   5   *Su. v. 2337*

The sun disappears with the day's decline
and darkness with the crescent moon;
beauty can by a twig be removed,
and asceticism by taking off the cloak.   6   *Su. v. 2346*

When the wedding rites of fools
are cancelled at the final stage,
they will then live by just pressing clothes,
like cows with water, but no fodder.   7   *Su. v. 2350*

You are one of the eight categories
of low classes: like singers, housemaids,
hill men, cheats, domestic servants,
whores, soldiers and barbarians.
If the boss again rebukes you,
what answer can your procurer give?   8   *Su. v. 2352*

My mother was not of a family high,
but my father was from a learned one,
and I their daughter, but more paternal.
Well, my sister, brother-in-law and nephew
were wrongly advised by others,
and then I was abandoned here,
both as a spouse, or even a mistress.   9   *Su. v. 2400*

O gallant, you see with all devotion
a pile of cooked meat, smelling of wine
prepared by slave girl dancers
at the mansion of that courtesan.
This is what her bawd arranges
daily for their god domestic—
an offering of lusty beasts
come there for that sacrifice.   10   *Su. v. 2376*

Don't hesitate, speak loudly
with a haughty face and seeming wisdom;
suddenly laugh with words obscene,
and then read out some arguments
that attract all those fools,
like a sage can do with ignorant folk
in those nice surroundings.   11   *Su. v. 2384*

First, when they were into trade,
with wealth like that of gods,
they were rather pompous then,
drunk with pride and arrogant,
given to grabbing others' riches,
and could also very cruel be.
But when their trade was ruined,
then beaten, their feet in chains,
faces lowered like an ascetic's,
these gentlemen seemed quite gracious. 12   *Su. v. 2405*

Here does sleep that mother old,
and there that ancient, aged father;
as for me, I was a call-girl,
now hired for hard work in this house.
Some days ago, my life's lord,
that traveller, did say to me,
'Why stay in this terrible place
with no return on your body's loan?'   13   *Su. v. 2247*

Your vow to stay in the forest did not
cause that lady's charming glances,
nor the end of her bodily glow,
not there in gold or even fire.   14   *Su. v. 2250*

When by nature in the hearts
of lovers is lit desire's flame,
why is it then dampened
with bad poems by deficient scholars?   15   *Su. v. 2232*

Canto 11

Subhashitavali (Su.)

Why do you, O maid, conceal
with both hands your face and bosom?
The lips and breasts of women do
look splendid with bites or scratches.   1   *Su. v. 1428*

On one side, your lips have marks
and even wounded seem to be.
O maid, you are for a battle suited,
not for work as a messenger.   2   *Su. v. 1430*

With a face wan, a gait lethargic
and pupils flickering in the eyes,
the voice unclear, the clothing unkempt—
O lady, do you have a fever?   3   *Su. v. 1433*

Below the brow, your earrings quiver
and cheeks turn pink, like trumpet flowers;
in making love, your body trembles,
O woman, it is like a flash of lightning.   4   *Su. v. 1435*

Whose arrival quickened your breath
and grace did make your body thrill?
Did your hair get loose and skirt drop down
to your feet with that coming too?
But now you seem to have been slighted—
your face is wet with perspiration
and lips look like a faded flower.
To whose words could this be due?   5   *Su. v. 1440*

Fair one, how did your girdle fall
on this road at night?
How come your face is covered with dust,
there is no make-up on it and
the colour from your lips is gone?
Was all this because of your sighs
when your clothes were taken off
by me with great temptation?   6   *Su. v. 1443*

Coming to you for what I sought,
there is this harsh wind on the way;
it is now tossing all your tresses
and of your hair making a mess.   7   *Su. v. 1444*

With my hands on both the cheeks,
since long my heart and eyes have been
just transfixed upon that person.
How can there be any room for pride?   8   *Su. v. 1381*

All the world it sees as empty
and claims it will be gone in a moment—
acting now against the scriptures,
has this mind into a Buddhist turned?   9   *Su. v. 1382*

A breeze perfumed by lily blooms
and echoing hums of bees and birds—
all this has been put together
by destiny for your destruction.   10   *Su. v. 1388*

That girl has eyes like lotus blossoms,
but with a look at her lovely loins
as she slept, I got, O friend,
a masculine feeling in my mind.   11   *Su. v. 1559*

Silently on the bed she sits,
her hair twisted in a braid,
and does meditate on him
for ensuring his protection—
that poor lady is thus engaged
in a fast for the god Pashupati.   12   *Su. v. 1392*

Smeared with the ash of sandalwood,
her forehead with tears anointed
and her breasts covered with lotus leaves,
she now fasts, as Kama advised,
because she does want you.   13   *Su. v. 1393*

Messenger girl, you have now done
a thing that is for others hard—
you have brought here a person who
ignores refuge, just seeks a hole.   14   *Su. v. 1432*

Your neck is sunk to the shoulder,
both your eyes are red,
the face has lost all colour.
O messenger girl, have you
now become a recluse?   15   *Su. v. 1526*

Canto 12

from SP, SM, SRB

By you I need to be remembered,
but I will not remember you,
for remembrance is in the mind,
and you have already stolen mine.   1   *SP v. 3391*

He does all rites of purification
and libations to ancestors,
but if these do never move his mind,
what for it can scriptures do?   2   *SP v. 4138*

Like ten wells is the water tank,
and like ten tanks the heart,
like ten hearts is a single son,
but this tree is like ten sons to me.   3   *SP v. 2086*

That tree in the cemetery
had gone dry since seven days,
but, softened by the piss and shit
of buffalos, now has lovely fruit.   4   *SP v. 2297*

With flesh of fish and fat of pigs,
some milk sprinkled and the heat,
it is strange, but all those seeds
have now become the fruit on trees.   5   *SP v. 2297*

If you are sick with scabs on limbs
and feeling hurt with too much phlegm,
but do wish to keep on living,
O then, there is cold water!   6   *SM 98.1*

That muscular traveller
is excited by the sighs
of that woman which do seem
like a gust of breeze that comes
from a host of lotus flowers.   7   *SM 98.8*

Her gaze is just like some red wine,
and the weight of breasts and hips
make her movements rather slow;
but, with fever due to Kama's arrows,
young men do suddenly stare at her.   8   *SM 98. 7*

That doe-eyed woman, with her breasts
round like the temples of an elephant,
embracing him within her house,
gives all joy to the boy-friend.   9   *SM 98.3*

From you I wish to drink some water,
O maiden with lotus eyes,
but cannot, if you are a slave;
if not, I will then drink it.   10   *SM 98.18*

Insects, ash or excrement
are to this body much attached;
to use them for tormenting another—
is that suitable behaviour?   11   *SRB SR v. 116*

Even having seen her body,
imperfect, untouched by air,
I indeed am quite straightforward
and do long to pierce through it.   12   *SRB SR v. 120*

That bit of skin, with two apertures
for taking in and letting off air—
the men who do enjoy it have
qualities like those of insects.   13 *SRB SR v. 123*

Spouses who do cause disgrace,
friends who to the prison lead
and pleasures that are poisonous—
these are enemies of the people,
and the folk attached by them
should not think they are well wished.   14 *SRB SR v. 126*

Her face is compared to the moon,
and eyes have won a host of men,
her breasts do look like rain clouds
with the lightning's glow,
but her body's terrible odours,
caused by pus and other fluids,
and the germs that are inside them
which also attract the flies—
these the people don't condemn.   15   *SRB SR v. 136*

Canto 13

from SM and Hasyarnava (HP2)

They pass by the lotuses of your eyes,
those pretty girls with painted toenails
and their heavy hips; but note
that they do think they will win your heart.   1   *SM (88) v. 1*

Garden, moonlight, songs and stories,
and your sport with a lovely girl
are results of serious efforts
that bring to earth the joys of heaven.   2   *SM (88) v. 4*

Every night and every day
with a terrible sound from her drum,
that one-eyed bride does look at the world,
putting it in a deep distress.   3   *SM (88) v. 7*

From another mouth, it is a curse,
but just a joke from one much loved;
it is like burning fuel or incense—
one leads to smoke, the other to fragrance. 4 *SM (88) v. 12*

Near one's love, silence is speech,
not looking is itself a gaze,
and taking off the cloak itself
is the offer of one's body.   5 *SM (88) v. 18*

At a drinking party, to behold
some wine entering that maiden's mouth
is like the moon being eclipsed
with the help of Kama, God of Love.   6   *SM (73) v. 7*

'Sir, do stop! Release my sash!'
and 'Girl-friend, turn off that lamp!'—
hearing these words of his new bride,
that youth has pleasure even more
than he could in copulation.   7   *SM (77) v. 4*

May those drops of perspiration,
produced during their intercourse
and dripping from that lady's face,
now upon his body fall.   8   *SM (79) v. 1*

From prayers to the ancestors
and adorations for the husband,
a woman gets only half of benefits,
the rest if she just listens to him.   9   *SM (118) v. 6*

To see the women of the house,
and eat there without distrust,
also to be told all secrets—
is there any greater friendship?   10   *SM (120) v. 5*

Refuge of all illness and disease,
I am that doctor, though not famous.
Instantly treated by me,
the great sage cannot stay alive.   11   *HP2 1 v. 31*

All the medicines may be there,
so too all the treatments,
but merely by seeing me,
life will leave that person ill.   12   *HP2 1 v. 32*

This is what the disease proclaims:
a paste, made by mixing scorpion stings
with thorny sand and applied to limbs,
will soon cure that itchy skin.   13   *HP2 1 v. 36*

Even gods have never tasted
the nectar of her lips,
that is why they quaff that vomit
of Rahu which does look like the moon. 14   *HP2 1 v. 49*

The orb of the sun about to set,
and that of the moon now rising—
both seem the angry blood-red eyes
of travellers looking for love.   15   *HP2 1 v. 46*

Canto 14

from HP2 and Chittavinodini (CV)

With saffron robes and an elegant club,
here he comes, that chief of rogues—
he fasts in the day, at night eats flesh,
has long hair, and looks for whores.   1   *HP2 1 v. 17*

Like round pitchers are the breasts
of that girl with doe-like eyes.
It will help if I can hold them
in crossing this sea, the world.   2   *HP2 1 v. 20*

Her eyes are closing for some sleep,
but glances twinkle still, like stars;
they are difficult to withstand,
even by that great god Shiva.   3   *HP2 2 v. 4*

Having both of shade and fruit,
a great tree should be put to use,
for if, by chance, there is no fruit,
who can take the shade away?   4   *CV p. 152*

Sipping the mango juice divine,
the cuckoo does not proud become,
but drinking dirty, muddy water,
the frog then does begin to croak.   5   *CV p. 337*

For learning science, give up pleasure,
in wanting pleasure, science forget;
but for pleasure-seekers, where is learning
or pleasure for those who want to learn?   6   *CV p. 114*

For a robber, where is religion?
Where is forgiveness for a wicked person?
For a prostitute, where is affection?
And where is truth for a lustful man?   7   *CV p. 224*

If one drinks milk at the end of day
and water at the end of night,
then after meals quaffs buttermilk,
where is the need for a doctor?   8   *CV p. 112*

O scentless flower, be not proud
if a little bee comes upon your crest,
for parted from its lotus blooms,
that big black bee will just finish you off.   9   *CV p. 112*

Do not serve a person low,
do this just for the best,
for from a vintner, even water
is better than that which seems to be a wine. 10   *CV p. 82*

The antelope's flesh, an elephants' tusk,
leather from deerskin, fruit from trees,
good looks in women, gold with men—
these merits can lead to enmity.   11   *CV p. 69*

In a mishap, what can sorrow do,
or pleasure in some success?
What has to happen, does take place—
that is the way of things.   12   *CV p. 83*

Crows don't make love in lotus pools,
nor swans in the water of a well;
fools like not to be near the wise,
or slaves beside a throne;
bad women avoid men who are good,
and also service by the low;
on feelings is one's nature based—
and that no one can change.   13   *CV p. 337*

One who just for beauty cares,
for flavour, fragrance, touch or sound,
or only for the act of sex—
what else does then for him remain?   14   *CV p. 69*

Wretches, dogs and those who are
just in eating food interested,
when indulged do come close by,
but shooed off will not go away.   15   *CV p. 96*

Bibliography

Sanskrit Texts

Karmarkar, R.D., ed. *Subhasitavali*. Bombay Sanskrit and Prakrit Series, 1961.

Peterson, P., ed. *Sarngadhara Paddhati*. Delhi: Chaukhamba Sanskrit Pratishthan, 1987.

Acharya, B.R., ed. *Subhasita Ratna Bhandagara*. Delhi: Munshiram Manoharlal Publishers, 1978.

Krishnamacharya, E., ed. *Sukti Muktavali of Jalhana*. Vadodara: Oriental Institute, 1991.

Other Works

Ghosh, N.N. *Early History of India*. Allahabad: Indian Press, 1948.

Keith, A.B. *A History of Sanskrit Literature*. Oxford University Press, 1961.

Winternitz, M. *History of Sanskrit Literature, Vol. III*, trans. Subhadra Jha. Delhi: Motilal Banarsidass Publishers, 1967.

Warder, A.K. *Indian Kavya Literature, Vol. VII*. Delhi: Motilal Banarsidass Publishers, 2004.